MRS PEPPERPOT
LEARNS TO SWIM

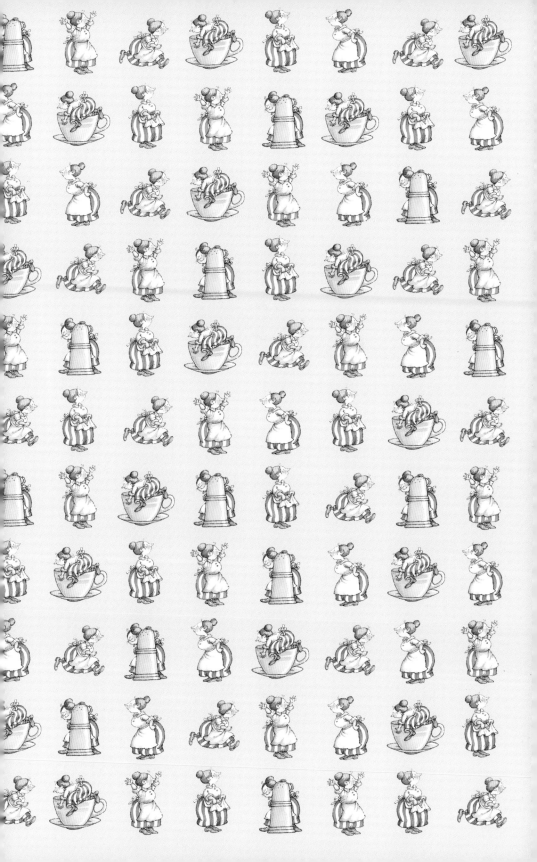

MRS PEPPERPOT LEARNS TO SWIM
A RED FOX BOOK 978 1 782 95356 2

First published in Great Britain by Hutchinson,
an imprint of Random House Children's Publishers UK
A Random House Group Company

Hutchinson edition published 2005
Red Fox edition published 2006
This Red Fox colour reader edition published 2014

1 3 5 7 9 10 8 6 4 2

Red Fox Books are published by Random House Children's Publishers UK,
61–63 Uxbridge Road, London W5 5SA

www.**randomhousechildrens**.co.uk
www.**randomhouse**.co.uk

Addresses for companies within The Random House Group Limited can be found at:
www.randomhouse.co.uk/offices.htm

THE RANDOM HOUSE GROUP Limited Reg. No. 954009

A CIP catalogue record for this book is available from the British Library.

Printed in China

The Random House Group Limited supports the Forest Stewardship Council® (FSC®),
the leading international forest-certification organisation. Our books carrying the FSC label
are printed on FSC® -certified paper. FSC is the only forest-certification scheme supported
by the leading environmental organisations, including Greenpeace. Our paper procurement
policy can be found at www.randomhouse.co.uk/environment

MIX
Paper from
responsible sources
FSC® C104723

MRS PEPPERPOT LEARNS TO SWIM

ALF PRØYSEN ❖ HILDA OFFEN

RED FOX

In the warm weather Mrs Pepperpot always walked through the wood when she went shopping. In the middle of the wood was a large pool where the village children swam. They splashed about and raced each other up and down.

Mrs Pepperpot always stopped to watch and she would sigh to herself and think, *If only I could do that!* Because nobody had taught her to swim when she was a little girl.

One day when she got home
she decided to practise
swimming in the kitchen.
She balanced herself on her
tummy on the kitchen stool
but when she flung out
her arms, she knocked a
saucepan of soup
off the stove!

Every night she would dream about
swimming. One night she dreamed she
could do the breaststroke. She stretched
forward her arms, bent her knees and
then – WHAM! – one foot almost kicked
a hole in the wall, the other knocked Mr
Pepperpot out of bed!

"What's the matter with you?" said Mr
Pepperpot.

"I'm swimming," answered Mrs
Pepperpot, who was still half in a dream,
"and it's the most wonderful feeling!"

"Well, it's not wonderful for me, I can
tell you!" said Mr Pepperpot crossly.

Then came a bright, warm day when all the village children were going on a picnic in the mountains.

That's good, thought Mrs Pepperpot. *There'll be no children in the pool today and I'll have a chance to learn how to swim.* And she walked through the wood to the pool.

It certainly looked inviting, with the sun shining down through the leaves and making pretty patterns on the still water.

She sat down on the soft grass and took off her shoes and stockings. Peering over the edge, she could see the water was very shallow so she stood up and said to herself, "All right, Mrs P, here goes!" And she jumped in.

But just at that moment, she SHRANK!

And now, of course, the pool seemed like an ocean to the tiny Mrs Pepperpot. "Help, help!" she cried.

"Hold on!" said a deep, throaty voice from below.

And a large frog swam smoothly towards her. "You should NEVER jump in a pool if you don't have someone with you," he said. "Now get on my back."

And he swam to a rock so Mrs Pepperpot could get her breath.

"You're a very good swimmer," said Mrs Pepperpot.

The frog puffed himself up importantly. "I'm the best swimming teacher in this pool," he said.

"D'you think you could teach *me* to swim?" asked Mrs Pepperpot.

"Of course. We'll begin right away,
if you like. Frogs are very good at
breaststroke. You climb on my back and
watch what I do."

Mrs Pepperpot watched how the frog
moved his arms and legs in time.

Then he found her
a little piece of
floating wood and
told her to hang
on. And she pushed
along with her legs,
just like the frog had
done.

After a while she
found herself
swimming along
without the piece
of wood.

"Yippee!" she
shouted with
excitement.

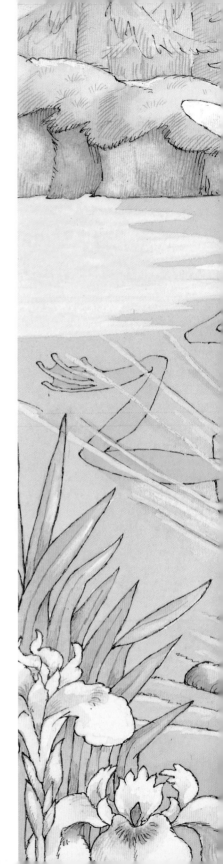

But the frog, who had been swimming close to her all the time, came up behind her and lifted her onto his back.

"That's enough for the moment," he said, and took her back to the rock for a rest.

Mrs Pepperpot was feeling so pleased with herself, she wanted to carry straight on and learn the crawl.

"Not so fast, my dear," the frog said.
"You must keep practising breaststroke
before you can do other things. But I'll
get my tadpoles to give you a show of
water acrobatics. How's that?"

"Wonderful!" said Mrs Pepperpot.

"Come on, children," he croaked. "I want you to show this lady all your best tricks."

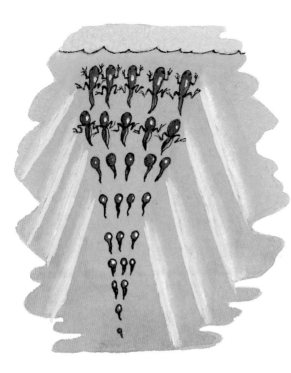

First the
tadpoles swam
to the top of the
water . . .

then they dived
to the bottom . . .

then they wove
in and out of
the reeds in a
beautiful
pattern.

And then,
like aeroplanes
doing
acrobatics, they
rolled over
and over and
looped
the loop.

The frog had puffed himself up so much he was nearly bursting with pride.

Mrs Pepperpot was just standing up to
cheer the tadpoles when she found herself
rolling about in what seemed more like
a large puddle than a deep pool; she had
GROWN!

As she picked herself up and waded out
of the water to the bank she could see
no sign of the frog or the tadpoles so she
hurried home.

A few days passed before Mrs
Pepperpot got a chance to go back to
the pool. But before she knew it she was
swimming along and she felt very proud.

Then she saw that she was being followed. There was the frog and behind him were all the tadpoles! The frog came to the top of the water and gave a loud croak.

"Thanks, Mr Frog," said Mrs Pepperpot. "You're the best swimming teacher in the world!"

"I told you so!" said the frog.

And with an elegant kick of his back legs, he did a nose-dive down into the pool and all the tadpoles followed after.